TYRONE
GOES TO SCHOOL

by Susan Saunders
and Steve Björkman

DUTTON CHILDREN'S BOOKS
New York

To Artemis Millan

S.S.

For Jack Green, who loved and believed
in children who draw, even during class

S.B.

Speedsters is a trademark of Dutton Children's Books.

Text copyright © 1992 by Susan Saunders
Illustrations copyright © 1992 by Steve Björkman

Library of Congress Cataloging-in-Publication Data

Saunders, Susan.
    Tyrone goes to school / by Susan Saunders and Steve Björkman.
       p. cm.
    Summary: When a boy takes his dog to obedience school, he
finds out something about his own learning ability.
    ISBN 0-525-44981-7
    [1. Learning—Psychology—Fiction.   2. Dogs—Training—Fiction.]
I. Björkman, Steve, ill.   II. Title.   92-14765
PZ7.S2577Ty   1992   CIP
[Fic]—dc20   AC

Published in the United States by Dutton Children's Books,
a division of Penguin Books USA Inc.
375 Hudson Street, New York, New York 10014

Printed in U.S.A.   First Edition
10 9 8 7 6 5 4 3 2 1

"Robert, Please Pay Attention!"

Ms. Wilmot is our teacher, and she is very strict.

If you say a few little words to a friend,

Ms. Wilmot prints your name on the board. It's so embarrassing!

If you make a quick sketch in your
notebook during math lesson—BAM!
Your name is up a second time.

If you barely peek out the window while someone else is reading, there she goes again.

In my class, three strikes and you're out—you've lost recess for a day.

I used to think Ms. Wilmot was too hard on us. But that was before Tyrone went to school.

Tyrone is my dog. He started out small.

But he ate and grew

and ate and grew . . .

Now Tyrone is about the size of a pony—
a pony covered with curly tan fur.

Things that were cute when he was a
puppy aren't so cute anymore . . .

like begging for food at the table

or barking like crazy
when the phone
rings

or jumping on Dad and knocking him
flat.

7

"Obedience classes might be a good idea," suggested my mom.

There were lots of listings in the Yellow
Pages. First we tried Quail Run Kennels.
But the lady at Quail Run asked a question
that we couldn't answer.

We only take
purebreds.
What kind of dog
is it?

What breed
is part poodle,
part Great Dane?
A doodle?
Or a pane?

Dad phoned Captain Jack's K-9 Boot Camp. I think Captain Jack wanted to turn poor old Tyrone into a marine.

V.I.P. Trainers come right to your house. But my dad said no. He could send me to college for what they would cost.

Finally we decided on group training for beginners, at the Reliable Obedience School.

Star Pupil

The next Saturday morning, I slipped a brand new collar around Tyrone's neck. I hooked up his new red leash. He looked great. Mom and I loaded him into the car and drove him to the Reliable Obedience School.

The trainer walked out to the parking lot to meet us. He was a tall guy with a big booming voice.

Tyrone started to jump up on Bud, just to say hello. Bud opened two humongous hands in front of Tyrone's face.

Tyrone stayed where he belonged, with all four paws on the ground. He wasn't going to mess with Bud.

15

Bud led us around the place to meet all the other students:

Maxine, a frisky golden Lab;

Zippy, a noisy fox terrier;

and Fred, a sleepy beagle.

"Today," said Bud, "the dogs will learn how to heel. If you teach your dog to heel—to stay by your side—you won't have to worry about him running out into traffic. It helps keep him safe."

He borrowed Tyrone to show us.

19

Bud stepped forward with his left foot.

Tyrone stepped forward too, as though he had known how to heel all his life.

Bud praised Tyrone.

Good boy!

"Your dog's nose should be even with your knee," he added.

Tyrone trotted along beside Bud with his nose in exactly the right place.

Bud barely had to touch Tyrone—he sat like a pro. Bud gave Tyrone a pat.

Then he handed me Tyrone's leash.

Everybody try it. Dog on the left.
End of the leash looped over the right
hand, left hand at about the
middle of the leash.
         Step forward.

Maxine was over-excited—she ran in circles. Her owner got so tangled in the leash that he couldn't move without help.

Fred yawned and peered sadly at his parked car. Then he lay down. He wanted to go home.

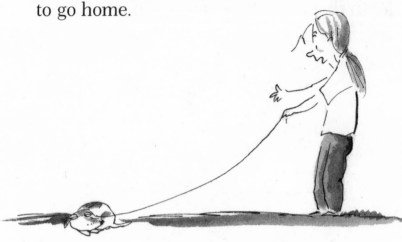

Zippy didn't go forward or backward. He went straight down. He dug a hole in the lawn that gave him a good start to China.

24

But Tyrone and I marched along like a drill team.

Tyrone stopped. Tyrone sat. He didn't miss a beat.

Maxine's owner was still unwinding himself. "It's easy to see who the star pupil is," he grumbled.

He meant Tyrone! I was really proud.

Soon the lesson was over.

Where had I heard those words before?
But Bud was still talking, so *I* had to focus.

I couldn't wait to show my dad how smart Tyrone was.

Problems at Home

When I got home, Dad asked me how the class went.

Dad came out to the backyard with us. I wanted to show him "heel" and "sit."

I hooked the leash to Tyrone's collar.

I lined him up with my left side.

I made sure his nose was even with my left knee.

"Heel, Tyrone,"
I said, and stepped
forward with my
left foot . . .

and Tyrone jumped straight
up in the air! He'd spotted
a butterfly.

Dad shook his head and sighed.

I got Tyrone settled and tried again.
"Heel, Tyrone," I said, louder this time.

I tugged on the leash and stepped
forward with my left foot . . .

and Tyrone began to bark so loud that my
ears hurt! The garbage truck was rattling
down our street, and Tyrone hates the
noise it makes.

Dad frowned. "If he doesn't stop that barking, we'll have Animal Control on our case!"

Sure, Dad. No problem.

But there was a problem.

A big problem.

Tyrone paid attention to Bud at the Reliable Obedience School. Bud was too big and too loud to ignore.

But I wasn't loud. I wasn't big. Tyrone sure wasn't paying attention to me in our own backyard.

I tried to boom it like Bud.

Then I stepped forward . . .

Tyrone shot in front of me. He hit the end
of the leash going about ninety miles an
hour. He was hot on the trail of Fluffy, the
neighbor's cat.

Both Tyrone and I piled into Dad. And that was the end of that lesson.

Later I gave Tyrone a serious pep talk. I
told him he'd better think things over and
mend his ways.

The next day, I tried again. But Tyrone wasn't any better. In fact, he was worse. That dog wouldn't listen to me at all.

He was too busy sniffing the air or scratching himself—or the ground—

or barking at every leaf that moved in the wind.

I yelled, I whistled, I stamped my feet. Tyrone hardly gave me a glance.

Finally I tried getting down on my hands and knees to look him in the eye. He washed my face with his tongue.

Then he lay down and took a nap.

If Tyrone didn't learn, Dad would be
unhappy. Very unhappy.

Maybe the next step would be . . . taking Tyrone back to the Community Pet Shelter? Or even . . . the Pound!

Ms. Wilmot's Advice

At school on Monday, I worried a lot about Tyrone. I guess it showed.

Ms. Wilmot called on me during reading. I lost my place—twice.

She sent me to the board during math. I worked my problem wrong—completely.

Ms. Wilmot asked us to pass our science homework to the front of the room. Mine was missing. I'd done it on Saturday—but I'd left it at home, on the kitchen table, along with my lunch.

Ms. Wilmot told me to see her after class.

"Is something bothering you?" she asked when I walked up to her desk.

"I'm having trouble with Tyrone," I said.

"Tyrone . . ." said Ms. Wilmot. "Do I know him?"

"No, Tyrone's my dog. He did fine at obedience school. Once we got home, though, he wouldn't pay attention to me. How can I teach him anything if he won't pay attention?"

"I know exactly what you mean," said
Ms. Wilmot.

"No," she said, "but I do have students."

I thought of our classroom. Sally Jane whispered, and she squirmed.

She reminded me of someone . . .
Maxine, the over-excited golden Lab!

Then I realized Mike Smith was a lot like Fred, the sleepy beagle. They both yawned all the time.

Josh Brown didn't exactly dig a hole in the ground, like Zippy the terrier. But he did dig through his backpack and his pockets and his desk.

And me? I guess I was sort of like Tyrone.

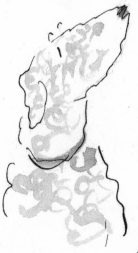

I didn't chase butterflies

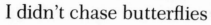

or cats.

But I definitely had problems *focusing*.

"Well," I said, "it wouldn't do any good to write Tyrone's name on the board. Or to keep him inside during recess."

I'd never heard of it.

"Drop five or six pennies into an empty soda can. Tape the hole closed, and every time you want to get Tyrone's attention, shake the can," said Ms. Wilmot.

Ms. Wilmot promised, "It never fails!"

Will It Work?

When I got home from school, I raced into the kitchen. We had plenty of empty soda cans, and a jar full of pennies.

I grabbed a can and dropped in seven pennies, for good luck.

I taped the can closed.

Then I hooked Tyrone's leash to his collar.

We headed for the backyard.

55

I put Tyrone on my left.

Instead of paying
attention, Tyrone twisted
around to bite at a flea.

I pulled the soda can out of my pocket and rattled it—loud.

Tyrone froze, the way he does when he hears the garbage truck. He stared at me and cocked his head.

I stopped rattling.

I stepped forward with my left foot. This
time Tyrone stepped forward too!

The soda can trick worked!

Every time Tyrone
started digging a hole

or barking at a bird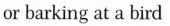

or chewing up
a pinecone,
I rattled the can.

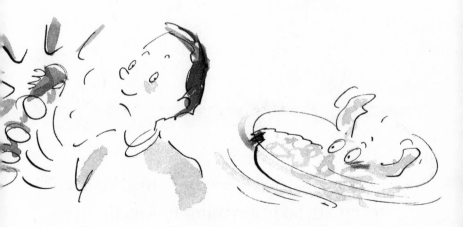

And every time, Tyrone paid
attention . . . and learned.

I had learned something too: You can't
teach anybody anything unless they pay
attention.

Which made me think of Sally Jane,

Mike Smith,

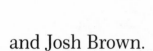

and Josh Brown.

And Andrew
and Nathaniel
and Jennifer.
And even me.

I wonder if the soda can trick would work in Ms. Wilmot's class?